Become a star reader w 🤚 W9-COP-561

This three-level reading series is designed for pre-readers, 10739-5286 beginning readers and is based on popular Caillou episodes. The books feature common sight words used with limited grammar. Each book also offers a set number of target words. These words are noted in bold print and are presented in a picture dictionary in order to reinforce meaning and expand reading vocabulary.

Level 1
Little Star

For pre-readers to read along
- 125-175 words
- Simple sentences
- Simple vocabulary and common sight words
- Picture dictionary teaching 6 target words

Level 2
Rising Star

For beginning readers to read with support
- 175-250 words
- Longer sentences
- Limited vocabulary and more sight words
- Picture dictionary teaching 8 target words

Level 3
Super Star

For improving readers to read on their own or with support
- 250-350 words
- Longer sentences and more complex grammar
- Varied vocabulary and less-common sight words
- Picture dictionary teaching 10 target words

Text: adaptation by Anne Paradis
Series Consultant: Rebecca Klevberg Moeller, Language Teaching Expert
All rights reserved.
Original story written by Sarah Margaret Johanson, based on the animated series CAILLOU
Illustrations: Eric Sévigny, based on the animated series CAILLOU

The PBS KIDS logo is a registered mark of PBS and is used with permission.

Chouette Publishing would like to thank the Government of Canada and SODEC for their financial support.

Books
Tax Credit

Gestion
SODEC

Bibliothèque et Archives nationales du Québec and Library and Archives Canada cataloguing in publication

Paradis, Anne, 1972-
Caillou: the bike lesson
New edition.

(Read with Caillou. Level 1)
Previously published as: Training wheels / Sarah Margaret Johanson.

For children aged 3 and up.

ISBN 978-2-89718-366-0

1. Caillou (Fictitious character) - Juvenile literature. 2. Cycling - Juvenile literature. I. Sévigny, Éric. II. Johanson, Sarah Margaret, 1968-   . Training wheels. III. Title. IV. Title: Bike lesson.

GV1043.5.P37 2017   j796.6   C2016-941542-2

Printed in China
10 9 8 7 6 5 4 3 2 1   CHO1955 FEB2017

The Bike Lesson

Text: Anne Paradis
Series Consultant: Rebecca Klevberg Moeller, Language Teaching Expert
Illustrations: Eric Sévigny, based on the animated series

chouette dhx media®

Caillou is going on a a **bike** ride.

His **bike** has training **wheels**.

Sarah rides with Caillou.
Her **bike** has no training **wheels**.

Daddy and Sarah are **fast**.

Caillou is **slow**.

Caillou wants to go **fast**.

Caillou wants to remove his training **wheels**.

Daddy removes the training **wheels**.

Daddy helps Caillou.

Daddy holds the **bike**.

The bike is **steady**. Caillou likes it.

Daddy runs a lot.
Daddy takes a break.

Caillou bikes by himself.

The **bike** is **wobbly**.
Caillou does not like it.

Daddy puts the **wheels** back on.

"Practice makes perfect," says Daddy.

Sarah is skating.

"Don't go too **fast**, Caillou.
Skating is hard."

Caillou says, "Practice makes perfect!"

Picture Dictionary

bike

wheels

fast

slow

steady

wobbly